Surprise Box

Nicki Weiss

G. P. Putnam's Sons New York

G. P. Putnam's Sons, a division of The Putnam & Grosset Book Group,
200 Madison Avenue, New York, NY 10016. Published simultaneously in Canada.
Printed in Hong Kong by South China Printing Co. (1988) Ltd.
Designed by Nanette Stevenson.

Library of Congress Cataloging-in-Publication Data
Weiss, Nicki, Suprise box / written and illusrated by Nicki Weiss.
p.   cm. Summary: A girl explores her surroundings both outdoors and
indoors, examining clover, ant, dandelion, and a surprise present.
[1. Gifts–Fiction.]   I. Title. PZ7.W448145Su   1991
[E] —dc20   90-8804   CIP   AC
ISBN 0-399-22210-3

1 3 5 7 9 10 8 6 4 2
First impression

For Suzanne and Michael and Zoe

Girl   Box

Ribbon   Drawer

Granny   Nap

Hallway   Door

Look

Kneel

Reach

Bend over

Twig

Dirt

Three-leaf clover

Pebble   Penny

Bottle cap   Nail

Ant

Worm

Frog

Snail

Weed   Grass

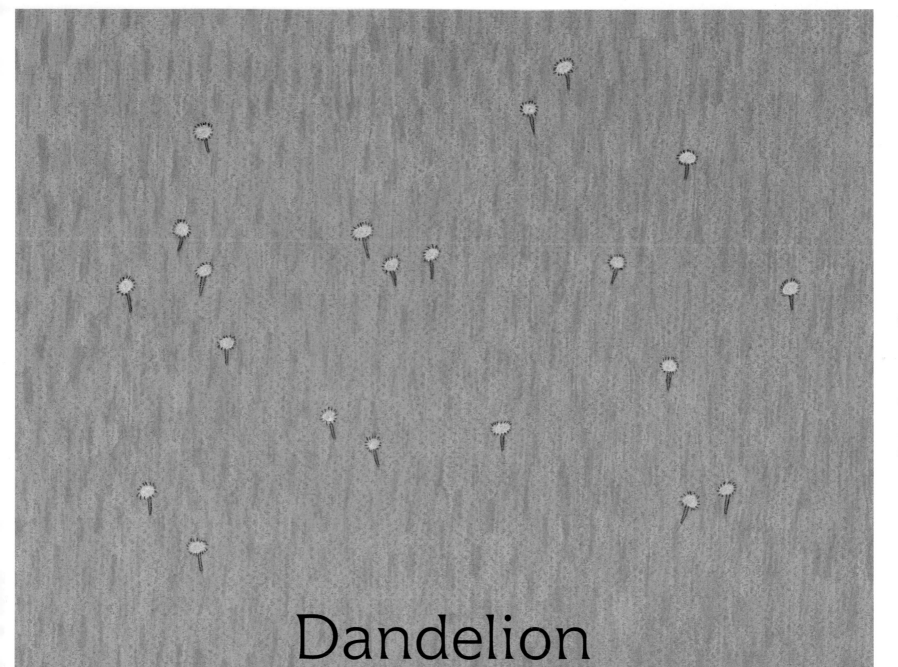

Dandelion

Three

Five

Seven

Nine !

Sit Wrap

Tie a bow

Open   Enter

Tiptoe

Surprise   Present

Sneak a peek

Shake

Listen

Stare

Shriek!

Wiggle   Crawl

Hop

Shrug

Girl   Granny

Giggle...

Hug!